AESOP'S FABLES

Selected and Illustrated by
Michael Hague

Holt, Rinehart and Winston
New York

Published by Holt, Rinehart and Winston,
383 Madison Avenue, New York, New York 10017.
Published simultaneously in Canada by Holt, Rinehart and
Winston of Canada, Limited.

Library of Congress Cataloging in Publication Data

Aesop's fables. English. Selections.
Aesop's fables.

Summary: The noted illustrator presents thirteen of
Aesop's most familiar fables.
1. Fables. [1. Fables]   I. Aesop.   II. Hague,
Michael, ill.   III. Title.
PZ8.2.A254   1985   398.2'452   84-19166
ISBN 0-03-002038-7

First edition
Printed in the United States of America
1 3 5 7 9 10 8 6 4 2

ISBN 0-03-002038-7

Contents

The Town Mouse and the Country Mouse

ONCE upon a time a Town Mouse went to visit an old friend who lived in the country. The Country Mouse was a plain, sensible sort of fellow and he welcomed the Town Mouse into his little home.

Beans and bacon and cheese and bread were all that the Country Mouse had to offer, but he offered them freely. The Town Mouse turned up his nose at the simple country food and said, "I cannot understand how you can bear the dullness of country life. You can't prefer the woods and fields to streets teeming with carriages and people. Come with me and I'll show you what *my* life is like." The Country Mouse agreed and they set out together that evening.

It was late in the night when the two mice crept into the great house where the Town Mouse lived. "You will want some refreshments after our long journey," said the Town Mouse as he led his friend into a grand dining room. On a huge table in the middle of the room were the remains of a splendid banquet. Soon the two mice were eating rare meats, fine cheeses, and delicious cakes.

In the middle of their feast the door flew open and a party of

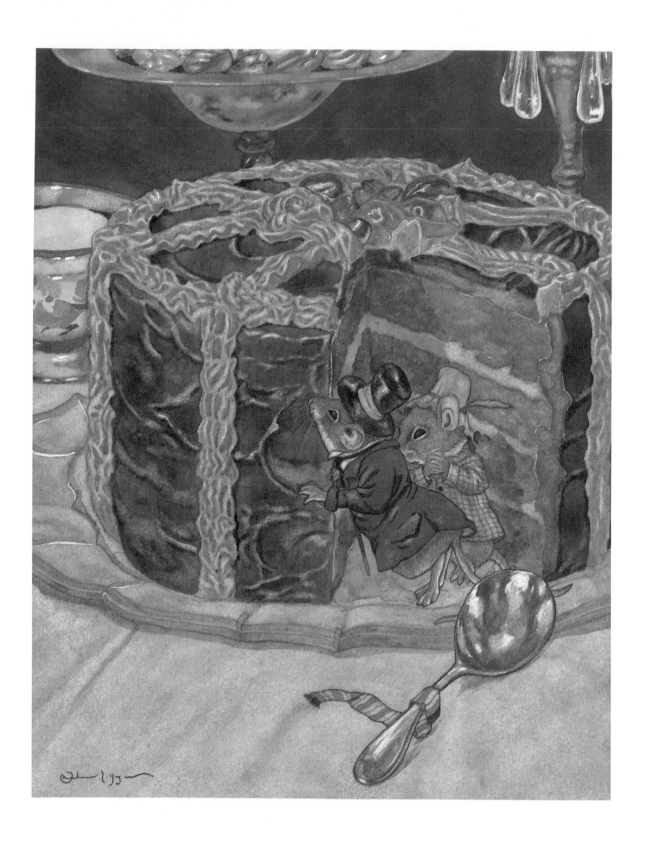

men and women entered. The frightened mice jumped from the table and scampered to the nearest hiding place. The mice clung to each other in terror until the party left. But as soon as they crept out again, the barking of a large dog drove them back in greater terror than before.

When the house was finally quiet, the Country Mouse scurried out from his hiding place. Bidding the Town Mouse good-bye, he said, "This life may be fine for you, but I would prefer beans and bacon in peace to cakes and ale in fear."

A simple life in peace and quiet is better than a
luxurious life tortured by fear.

The Lion and the Mouse

A mighty Lion was sleeping in his lair when he was awakened by a tiny Mouse running across his body. The Lion grabbed the frightened creature with his huge paws and opened his mouth to swallow him. "Please, O King," cried the Mouse, "spare me this time and I shall never forget your kindness. Someday I may be able to repay you." The Lion was so amused by this idea that he let the poor creature go.

Sometime later the Lion was caught in a net laid by some clever hunters. Despite his great strength, the Lion could not break free. Soon the forest echoed with angry roars.

The little Mouse heard the Lion and ran to see what was wrong. As soon as he saw the Lion, he began to gnaw away the ropes, and before long he set the Lion free. "There!" said the Mouse proudly, "You laughed at me when I promised to repay your kindness, but now you know that even a tiny Mouse can help a mighty Lion."

Little friends may prove to be great friends.

The Fox and the Goat

A Fox had fallen into a well from which he could not get out. After a while a thirsty Goat walked by and asked the Fox if the water was good. "Good?" said the Fox. "It's the best water I ever drank in all my life. Come down and try it yourself." The Goat was so thirsty that she jumped in at once. The clever Fox immediately climbed on the Goat's back, and by putting his feet on her long horns managed to pull himself out of the well.

"Good-bye, my friend," said the Fox as he walked away. "If you had any sense you wouldn't have jumped into the well without making certain that you could get out again."

Look before you leap.

The Cat and the Birds

A Cat heard that the Birds in an aviary were sick. So he dressed himself up as a doctor, and, taking with him a set of instruments proper to his profession, rang the door-bell, and inquired about the health of the Birds. "We shall feel much better," they replied, without letting him in, "when we've seen the last of you."

A villain may disguise himself, but he will not deceive the wise.

The Crow and the Pitcher

A thirsty Crow came upon a pitcher that was half full of cool, clear water. The Crow tried to take a drink, but his beak was not long enough. He tried over and over again, and was about to give up in despair when he hit upon a plan. One by one, he began dropping pebbles into the pitcher. With each pebble the water rose a little higher until at last it reached the brim, and the clever bird quenched his thirst.

Necessity is the mother of invention.

The Mice in Council

Long ago the Mice held a council to consider what measures they could take to outwit their common enemy, the Cat. Many plans were discussed and rejected when, at last, a young Mouse stood up and said, "I think I have a plan that will ensure our safety. You will all agree that the chief danger is the sly, quiet manner in which the Cat approaches us. I therefore propose that a small bell be attached around the Cat's neck. This way we will always know when the Cat is approaching."

This plan was warmly applauded, until a wise old mouse stood up and said, "I agree with everyone that the plan is very clever, but who is going to put the bell on the Cat?"

It is easy to propose impossible solutions.

The Marriage of the Sun

ONE very warm summer, the animals learned that the Sun was going to be married. All the birds and beasts were delighted to hear the news. The Frogs, more than anyone else, were determined to celebrate the occasion with a festival of singing and dancing. But a wise old Frog put a stop to the festivities by pointing out that it was an occasion for sorrow, rather than for joy. "If the Sun dries up our beloved marshes now," said the Frog, "what will happen when he has children?"

It is possible to have too much of a good thing.

The Hare and the Tortoise

ONE day a quick-footed Hare was making fun of a slow-moving Tortoise. Much to the Hare's surprise, the Tortoise began to laugh. "I challenge you to a race," said the Tortoise, "and I bet that I will win."

"Very well," said the Hare, "I will dance rings around you all the way."

It was soon agreed that the Fox would set the course and be the judge. The race began and the Hare ran so quickly that he soon left the Tortoise far behind. Once he reached the middle of the course, the Hare decided to take a nap.

While the Hare slept, the Tortoise plodded on and on, straight toward the finish line. When the Hare awoke from his nap, he was surprised that the Tortoise was nowhere in sight. Racing to the finish line as fast as he could, the Hare was shocked to find the Tortoise waiting for him with a smile on his face.

Slow and steady wins the race.

The Wolf and the Kid

A young Kid was returning from the pasture one day when he was seen by a Wolf. The Wolf began to chase the helpless Kid, who soon realized that he could not escape. The Kid stopped running and when the Wolf came near he said, "I know, dear Wolf, that I am now your prey. But if my life must be short I want it to be merry. Will you play me a tune so that I may dance before I die?"

The Wolf took out his little pipe and played a merry tune while the Kid danced on his two hind legs. Across the field the Dogs heard the music and ran up to see what was going on. Seeing the Dogs, the foolish Wolf ran away as fast as his legs could carry him, leaving the Kid behind.

He who plays the fool should not be surprised
if he misses the prize.

The Fox and the Grapes

ONE hot summer's day a Fox was strolling through an orchard, when he saw a bunch of ripe grapes hanging on a vine trained over a lofty branch. "Just the thing to quench my thirst," said the Fox.

Stepping back a few paces, the Fox jumped high in the air, but just missed the grapes. Turning around he jumped up with all his strength, but once again missed. Again and again he tried to reach the luscious grapes. Finally, he became so hot and so tired that he gave up. Walking away with his nose in the air, the Fox said, "I don't want those grapes, I am sure they are sour."

It is easy to despise what you cannot obtain.

The Ass in the Lion's Skin

AN Ass once found a Lion's skin that some hunters had left out in the sun to dry. He put it on and trotted through the forest and meadow scaring all the poor animals.

The Ass was so proud of himself that he raised his head and brayed loudly in triumph. But a Fox heard him and recognized him at once. "I'm very sorry, my friend," said the Fox, "but even though you may pretend to be a Lion, you are still an Ass."

Do not pretend to be something that you are not.

The Fox and the Crow

A big black Crow was sitting on a branch of a tree with a piece of cheese in her beak, when she was seen by a hungry Fox.

The Fox walked under the branch, looked up at the Crow, and said, "What a noble bird you are! Your beauty is without equal and the color of your feathers is exquisite. If your voice is as sweet as your looks, then I think you are the Queen of the Birds." The Crow was very flattered by the Fox's compliments and, just to show him that she could sing, she opened her mouth to caw. But as soon as she opened her mouth, the cheese fell to the ground, where it was snatched up by the clever Fox.

Do not trust flatterers.

The Cock and the Jewel

A Cock was once strutting back and forth in the farmyard, looking for food for the Hens, when he saw a jewel shining in the dirt. "Ho! Ho!" said the Cock. "You may be a treasure to men who prize you, but I would rather have one grain of delicious barley than all the jewels in the world."

Precious things are for those who prize them.

Composition: Waldman Graphics, Inc., Pennsauken, New Jersey
Color Separations: Offset Separations Corporation, Turin, Italy
Offset Printing and Binding: Krueger, New Berlin, Wisconsin

Designer: Marc Cheshire
Production Editors: Harriet Sigerman and Trent Duffy
Production Manager: Karen Gillis